THIS IS WHERE WE GET OFF

INGRAM NOBLE & HEATHER SPIDEN

Ingram Noble was born in 1998. He grew up in the North East of England and the East End of Glasgow. Ingram went on to receive an 'Achieving Diversity' award from the Glasgow Regional College Board for his contribution to the award-winning piece, *'This Restless Life.'* In 2020 Ingram began hosting the Theatre Podcast, *'Drama School Dropout'* which has gone on to find huge success. Heather Spiden was born in 1997 and grew up on the Isle of Skye before moving to Glasgow to study acting at Glasgow Kelvin College. After receiving her HND she went onto continue her studies at the University of the West of Scotland. She has starred in many plays including playing *Banquo* in *Macbeth,* as well as starring in many other plays such as *Dracula* and *Muddy Cows* by John Godber. In 2018 Heather starred in the musical, *'The Producers'*. Heather has always had a keen interest in script writing and recently decided to focus her efforts on this. In 2020 during the Coronavirus pandemic, she published her first play *'This Is Where We Get Off'*.

Note for Producers

Publication of this play does not imply availability for performance. Both amateurs and professionals considering a production are strongly advised in their own interest to apply to Ingram Noble at info.hiproductions1@gmail.com for written permission before starting rehearsals, advertising or booking a theatre.

<u>Important Billing and Credit Notes:</u>
All producers of 'THIS IS WHERE WE GET OFF' must give credit to the authors (Ingram Noble and Heather Spiden) in all programmes distributed in connection with the performance of the play, and in all instances in which the title of the play appears for the purposes of advertising.

Any and all artwork that appears on or in this book remains the direct property of Ingram Noble and Heather Spiden. Please do not reproduce without written permission.

This is a work of fiction. Names, characters, places, and incidents either are products of the authors' imagination or are used fictitiously. Any resemblance to actual persons, living or dead, or events is entirely coincidental.

First paperback edition May 2020

ISBN 9798648702929 (paperback)

10 9 8 7 6 5 4 3

<u>Original Cast</u>

This Is Where We Get Off was first performed at The Webster's Theatre in Glasgow on April 21st, 2022 directed by Ingram Noble and Heather Spiden, with the following cast:

Yvonne..Laura Begley
Phillip............….............................…..Robert McCahill
Lip.......................….............................Josh Knowles
Sylvia...…..Freda Macdonell
Rhonda.............…...........................…...Leah Moorhouse
Nicky..........................….…...............…Heather Spiden

Crew:

Directors: Ingram Noble and Heather Spiden
Stage Manager: Angela Gascoine

THIS IS WHERE WE GET OFF

Written and Created by

Ingram Noble and Heather Spiden

"Do not ask me to remember,
don't try to make me understand.
Let me rest and know you're with me,
kiss my cheek and hold my hand.

I'm confused beyond your concept,
I'm sad and sick and lost.
All I know is that I need you,
to be with me at all cost.

Do not lose your patience with me,
do not scold or curse or cry.
I can't help the way I'm acting,
I can't be different though I try.

Just remember that I need you,
that the best of me is gone.
Please don't fail to stand beside me,
Love me 'til my life is gone."

- Owen Darnell

For Isa & Jean

The Playwrights' Notes

This play, for the most part was written during the 2020 Coronavirus pandemic. We would like to thank our friends Gabby Burdess, Aidan Coulter, Anna Davidson, Chloë Johnson, Jack Mair, Robert McCahill, Conor Patrick, Holly Prowse, Emma Sinclair, and Kelsey Wilson who all banded together to help us develop this play over Zoom video chats.

We would also like to thank the people who came to our rescue and modelled socially distant to appear on the cover: Jack Mair, Robert McCahill and Elizabeth Snowden.

And to the first cast that are coming together during the 2021 lockdown to produce a rehearsed reading to raise money to produce the show in a theatre, as well as the countless people who auditioned. Thank you for bringing our people to life!

We would also like to thank Leah Moorhouse, who directed the play, Macbeth where we both first met; and Angela Gascoine, our first ever stage manager.

Rehearsed Reading Cast:
Phillip: Robert McCahill
Yvonne: Angela Stone
Lip: Andrew Houghton
Sylvia: Lynne Whitaker
Rhonda/Nicky: Chantelle Hooley

PRAISE FOR 'THIS IS WHERE WE GET OFF'

"A confident, hilarious play full of truth and heart - I loved it!" – Susan Nickson, the creator of Two Pints of Lager and a Packet of Crisps.

"A rip roaring off the wall comedy with a deep gut punch of an ending." – Parry Glasspool, actor (Hollyoaks).

*"A proper slice of life balancing comedy and tragedy. Equal parts hilarious and devastating!"
– Ethan Lawrence, actor (Bad Education).*

"To its absolute credit, This Is Where We Get Off transcends the broader media obsession with depicting working-class people as one-dimensional characters for a cheap laugh or weak Soap Opera plot. It has bags of charm, character, smarts and wit. Its moral goes deeper than you'd expect and drags you into the orbit of chaos that makes up the Moffatt's lives." – Binge Fringe Magazine.

CHARACTERS

PHILLIP MOFFATT, *early forties.*

YVONNE MOFFATT, *mid-forties.*

LIP MOFFATT, *eighteen.*

RHONDA, *late thirties.*

SYLVIA, *early sixties.*

NICKY, *late twenties.*

<u>Notes for Performance</u>

- The play takes place in the North of England.
- The initial location, day, and time of each scene is stated at the beginning of the scene.
- During the performance, one of the wings on stage should represent the front door of the house and used as the main entrance and exit and the other wing should be used as an extension to other rooms in the house (the bathroom etc.).
- The stage should resemble a kitchen and a living room.
- Bricklethwaite is pronounced [Brick-ill-thwait].

This text went to press before the end of rehearsals, so it may differ slightly from the play as performed.

Prologue
Saturday Night.

*(*PHILLIP *is sitting on the edge of the stage, as if he's leaning against the back door of the house. It's evident that he's drunk. He's clutching a can of lager.)*

PHILLIP: *(To the audience.)* Who the fuck are you lot? Can't you see the sign outside? Grandad's dead, so we haven't got a telly, so we haven't got a licence for one, alright? Now, piss off! – Not here about the telly licence? Alright – anyway, moving on. Welcome to Bricklethwaite. I am Phillip, Lord of the Manor. My wife, she's Yvonne. My son, he's Lip, that's short for Phillip; named him after me we did. Then you've got the neighbours. Rhonda and Gary. Dog breeders. Haven't done a weekly shop in their life. But, decent people, decent place, you know? *(*PHILLIP *laughs.)* Would you care to join me? *(A pause.* PHILLIP *gestures for the audience to join him in bringing their hands together in prayer. He's being extra careful not to spill his lager as he makes his way onto the stage.)* Our father, who art in Heaven. Howard be thy name. Thy kingdom come; thy will be done on earth as it is in heaven. Give us this day our daily bread and forgive us our trespasses as we forgive those who trespass against us and lead us not into temptation but deliver us from evil. For thine is the kingdom, and the power, and the glory, forever. Amen.

(There is a harsh and instant blackout on the word 'Amen'.)

Scene One
Sunday. 11AM. The Kitchen.

(As the lights come up, a heavily pregnant YVONNE *is sitting at the kitchen table and pulls an envelope out of her handbag. She starts writing on the back of the envelope. There should also be a full washing basket on the kitchen table. The radio is playing.)*

RADIO: Welcome to Clitoral FM, the best female radio station, because the men can't find it. Coming up on today's show, why keeping your dildo in the fridge might bring a whole new meaning to chilling out.

*(*YVONNE *turns the radio off.)*

YVONNE: Shopping List. Hello! Anybody home? – Phil? – Lip? Anyone in?

*(*PHILLIP *enters, in a pair of boxers and a stained vest. He goes straight to the fridge and produces a can of beer.)*

YVONNE: It's not even twelve yet.

PHILLIP: Hello, Yvonne. Good morning, Yvonne. How are you, Yvonne?

YVONNE: I'm going down the shop. Do you want anything?

*(*PHILLIP *gestures with his can of beer.* YVONNE *adds beers to the list.)*

PHILLIP: And fags. Twenty fags. Oh, and a razor.

(She adds them to the list.)

YVONNE: Anything else?

PHILLIP: You going down the Precinct or Asda?

YVONNE: Katrina's. – I need to go down to the chemist too, to pick up Lip's prescription. He's ran out of inhalers.

PHILLIP: It's a bloody joke, I tell ya! Having to pay for a prescription so the boy can breathe. That's the NHS for you! I told you we would've been better off in Glasgow!

YVONNE: What? Land of the sheep shaggers and men wearing skirts?

PHILLIP: I keep telling you, Scotland isn't Wales.

*(*RHONDA *enters.)*

RHONDA: Hello Yvonne, love. It's only me.

PHILLIP: Alright Rhonda?

RHONDA: Hiya, Phil! How ya doing?

PHILLIP: Good, good. Aye, I'm good.

(This whole speech from RHONDA *takes place with* RHONDA's *head in the fridge.)*

RHONDA: I was wondering; I know I'm a nightmare, but could I possibly steal your butter for five minutes? I was just making some toast, and I saw that the dogs have got into the fridge again. Absolutely destroyed the butter and half a dozen Müller Corner yogurts!

(She resurfaces with butter and a left-over takeaway container. She grabs a fork and starts eating the leftovers.)

PHILLIP: *(Sarcastically.)* Nightmare.

YVONNE: Of course, take whatever you need.

RHONDA: You're a star. Honestly, I don't know what I'd do without you all!

PHILLIP: Do your own weekly shop?

(YVONNE kicks PHILLIP under the table. RHONDA helps herself to the butter. PHILLIP goes to stand.)

PHILLIP: Wishing you all the best, Rhonda. I really do. But it's time for Richard and Judy.

RHONDA: Right, I'll be off! Gary will be gasping for his beans on toast. He's been up all night. You know, he was doing that sponsored event with the boys last night. He was doing a round-the-clock pancake flip for all of the little folk in the area that have a fear of buses. Poor little mites shit themselves at the sight of a number forty-one. – I'll see you in a few hours, Yvonne.

PHILLIP: See ya!

RHONDA: Bye.

(RHONDA exits. There's a moment of silence. PHILLIP takes a swig from his can of lager.)

PHILLIP: Butter.

YVONNE: Butter?

PHILLIP: Add it to your list. She's no bringing that one back.

YVONNE: Will you go and get dressed?

PHILLIP: Will you let a man wake up? It's a Sunday. God's day of rest!

YVONNE: Well, what's your excuse for the rest of the week? – Dressed. Now.

(PHILLIP exits. YVONNE goes back to her shopping list.)

YVONNE: Butter, beers, fags, pizzas, flavoured condoms. Milk, shampoo, bread, bog roll, toothpaste, the cheap custard creams Lip likes. And a black marker pen for the scuff on my heels?

(LIP enters in his football kit, holding a leaflet.)

LIP: Alright Mam?

YVONNE: Morning son. Where've you been?

LIP: Football.

(LIP reads her shopping list.)

LIP: Condoms? It's a bit late for that, don't you think?

YVONNE: They're not for me, or your father. They're for you. You've been seeing a lot of that – what's her name again?

LIP: Rosie.

YVONNE: We've already got a little one on the way. I don't think this house could deal with two screaming babies.

LIP: And sherbet flavour? What is wrong with you?

YVONNE: It's the nicest flavour. Your father loves a dib dab.

LIP: Me and Rosie – we're just…

YVONNE: Shagging?

LIP: What? You can't be saying stuff like that!

YVONNE: Lip, son. You're getting to that age. You're bound to be, you know…

LIP: I'm not having this conversation with you.

YVONNE: You've broken three beds in the past two years! Do you not think your father and I didn't click onto the fact that you were going at it like rabbits? – It's nothing to be ashamed of! It's perfectly natural!

LIP: Jesus Christ!

YVONNE: Do you want anything from the shop?

LIP: Some dignity?

YVONNE: Don't be so silly. I'm your mam! If you can't talk to me about your sex life, then who can you talk to about it?

LIP: Anyone else. Literally anybody else.

(YVONNE *notices a leaflet in* LIP's *hand.)*

YVONNE: What's that?

LIP: Nothing. It's nothing.

(LIP *tries to get rid of the leaflet.)*

YVONNE: No, no. Give it here.

(YVONNE *grabs the leaflet.)*

LIP: Mam, it's nothing.

YVONNE: The army? You're not thinking of joining up, are you?

LIP: No!

YVONNE: Don't lie to me!

LIP: Maybe. – Would you be bothered?

YVONNE: Bothered? You've been an absolute dead weight since you turned sixteen.

LIP: What?

YVONNE: Since the child benefit stopped. You've been useless ever since. The only good thing about this little 'un on the way is the sixty quid a month in child benefit.

(YVONNE *starts folding the washing.*)

LIP: I contribute to the family pot!

YVONNE: Twenty quid a week!

LIP: Most of my fucking wages!

YVONNE: And how far do you think that twenty quid goes?

LIP: You know, the best thing I could do is join the army and get away from you lot.

YVONNE: Go on then! If you want rid of us so bad! Get out! And take your money with you.

(YVONNE *takes a twenty pound note out of her bra and throws it at* LIP.)

LIP: Listen, "Mam". I'm only here until…

YVONNE: What? Until you save up enough to buy your own house?

LIP: No, until I save up enough money to put you in a fucking care home!

YVONNE: Charming! – Well, at least I'll know that I'll be looked after in my old age. *(YVONNE strikes the condoms off her list.)* Sort out your own contraception from now on then. Let's see how well you cope without your mam catering for your every need.

LIP: Mam? Are you having a laugh? You've not done enough to be called that.

YVONNE: Not done enough? I carried you for nine months! I raised you and you're still standing here with a roof over your head and clothes on your back.

LIP: Hip, hip fucking hooray!

(LIP takes his football top off.)

LIP: Where do you want this?

YVONNE: On the table. Shorts too, I'll put them on a boil.

(LIP drops the shorts to the floor and YVONNE hands him some fresh clothes from a pile of washing on the kitchen table. He gets dressed. The doorbell rings and LIP goes to answer it.)

YVONNE: Tell whoever that is to fuck off! And you can follow them!

LIP: This is my house.

YVONNE: Purely by the good grace of yours truly.

(*LIP turns to face the door.*)

LIP: Who are you?

SYLVIA: *(Off-stage.)* I could say the same to you! This is Yvonne's house.

LIP: In there.

(*LIP exits.*)

YVONNE: Lip! My twenty quid!

LIP: *(Off-stage.)* Fuck off!

(*SYLVIA enters, she's clutching her handbag. She looks lost and confused.*)

SYLVIA: Charming young man. – Back in my day, if a young lad spoke like that to their elders, they'd have swiftly been put across someone's knee.

YVONNE: Mam?

SYLVIA: Hello Yvonne. – Who was that? The lodger?

YVONNE: Mam, that was Lip – Phillip. Your grandson!

(*SYLVIA doesn't remember.*)

SYLVIA: Of course. Phillip. *(A Pause.)* Hello Yvonne.

YVONNE: What're you doing here? I thought you were in Portugal?

SYLVIA: Portugal? I never left Plymouth.

YVONNE: Plymouth? PLYMOUTH? Are you having a laugh? What is wrong with you?

SYLVIA: Sorry, Yvonne love. Just couldn't be arsed with you really.

YVONNE: All of this time and you've only been a couple of hours down the road? You've never even met your grandson!

SYLVIA: I sent the boy some premium bonds!

YVONNE: That's not the point, mother.

SYLVIA: Grow up, Yvonne.

YVONNE: What do you think I've been doing all these years? I've been running a household!

SYLVIA: Running a household? You're still a little girl!

YVONNE: I am thirty-eight years old!

SYLVIA: Silly teenage girl. Hormones running wild. Having me running all over the place coming to dig you out of whatever hole you've gotten yourself into.

YVONNE: THIRTY-FUCKING-EIGHT, MOTHER!

SYLVIA: Watch your mouth, lady! Any more of that and I'll call for your father!

YVONNE: Dad's dead, being married to you drove him to the drink.

SYLVIA: You're a selfish, wicked girl; telling lies like that, trying to send me 'round the bend. You'll get it for this, Lady! You've gone too far this time!

(SYLVIA walks over to YVONNE. SYLVIA is clearly trying to intimidate YVONNE.)

YVONNE: You don't scare me anymore, mother.

SYLVIA: Too easy on you, I was. Should've gave you a few more whacks with your father's belt.

YVONNE: A few more?

SYLVIA: You go on like you were beat like one of the kids on the NSPCC adverts.

YVONNE: I wasn't far off it.

(PHILLIP enters, he's dressed and still drinking from his can of lager.)

PHILLIP: Yvonne, love. What's for breakfast? I'm starving. *(He has to double take as he sees SYLVIA.)* Oh, hello, Sylvia. What are you doing here? – How's Portugal?

YVONNE: Plymouth. And nothing. You'll have to sort yourself out, the fridge is empty.

PHILLIP: Plymouth – Portugal. Tom-ay-toe, tomato. – Yvonne, a word. *(PHILLIP motions with his head for her to join him and she does. They walk away, out of* SYLVIA*'s earshot.)* What is Daffy Duck doing here?

YVONNE: I don't know. Lip's going off to Afghanistan, and then *she* turned up on the doorstep!

PHILLIP: Afghanistan? Right, lets deal with one silly wee fucker at a time, shall we?

YVONNE: There's something wrong with her.

PHILLIP: Like what? She's always been a few pence short of a pound. Get her to fuck.

YVONNE: I can't just throw her out, she's my mother.

PHILLIP: A shit excuse for one. After she let Michael do what he did to you.

YVONNE: She's still my mother, and there's something wrong with her. I'm worried about her, Phillip.

PHILLIP: Come on, Yvonne. Take your head out your arse. She's never cared about you!

YVONNE: Phillip…

PHILLIP: Well, she hasn't, has she? What's changed? Get rid of her. I'm off down the pub.

YVONNE: Can you not stay and help me? I need to figure out what we're going to do.

PHILLIP: Absolutely not. You know what she does to me. Five minutes with Daffy Duck and I'll be the one who needs committing to the psychiatric unit. – See you later.

(PHILLIP kisses YVONNE on the cheek and goes to exit.)

SYLVIA: Oh, you off Phillip?

PHILLIP: Back off down the mine. Dinner breaks done. You know, no rest for the wicked.

(YVONNE walks over to PHILLIP. They're out of SYLVIA's earshot.)

YVONNE: What are you doing, Phillip? The mine's been shut for years.

PHILLIP: Well, Looney Tunes over there doesn't know that, does she? I'm serious, Yvonne. Have her out by the time I get home. – Bye Sylvia. See you next time.

(PHILLIP exits.)

SYLVIA: I can never understand what he's saying.

(There is a change in SYLVIA.)

SYLVIA: I've booked myself a room for a couple of weeks. You see, my daughter is about to have a little baby, and I looked on the Google and thought your hotel was ideal. – Yes. A nice hotel for a couple of weeks stay so I can get my girl through the last bit of her pregnancy. She's an old bird, you see. She's nearly fifty. Still a silly, little slapper mind. Daft enough to get pregnant again. What idiot wants two kids?

YVONNE: SHUT UP MOTHER!

SYLVIA: You're no daughter of mine.

YVONNE: Well, we always knew that. As soon as I fell out of your womb you couldn't bear to look at me!

SYLVIA: Listen, fat fuck!

YVONNE: I am seven months pregnant.

SYLVIA: Listen, lady! Speak to me like that once more and I'll have my daughter come over to this glorified hostel you call a hotel and give you a good hiding.

YVONNE: Phillip's right! You've lost the plot!

SYLVIA: You stay away from Phillip! That's my girl's fella. They're due to get wed.

YVONNE: We've been married for twenty years.

SYLVIA: You're not married to Phillip! Him and my Yvonne, they've got a good thing. They've got a little nipper on the way. – I won't let you ruin what they've got going, you spiteful bitch!

YVONNE: Mother!

SYLVIA: Stop calling me that. You're sick.

YVONNE: What's wrong with you? Mam, it's me, Yvonne.

SYLVIA: No, no. Not my Yvonne. No, no. Not my Yvonne. My Yvonne is skinny and beautiful.

YVONNE: Maybe once upon a time.

SYLVIA: No, she is. *(There's a change in* SYLVIA.*)* Do you happen to know where forty-three North Road is?

(A pause.)

YVONNE: This is forty-three North Road.

(Another pause.)

SYLVIA: You know what, why don't I make us a nice brew?

YVONNE: There's no milk.

SYLVIA: Well, we better go and get some then.

YVONNE: It's on my list.

SYLVIA: Good. List, ay? Good on you. Just shows that you're running a proper household. Not like some of these council estate mams who just wander around Asda buying loads of those what-d'ya-ma-call-'ems? My kids never got any of those. Kinder eggs, comics, none of that. – I should've given her something though. You know, in addition to the odd smack. – God, she was a handful.

YVONNE: A handful?

SYLVIA: That she was! I couldn't get a moment's peace. Always some sort of drama. If my Yvonne was there, there was guaranteed to be some sort of drama.

YVONNE: Drama?

SYLVIA: Trouble more like.

YVONNE: How would you know? You couldn't even be bothered to pull yourself out of the Tyneside Tavern to see if I'd had a wash.

SYLVIA: Always some sort of trouble when it comes to that girl. So nasty sometimes. You know, she told me once, after her father died that this fella I was seeing at the time – Michael – his name was…

YVONNE: I don't need to hear anymore.

SYLVIA: Bit of a prude, are you?

YVONNE: Not at all, it just sounds like your daughter would want whatever she told you to stay between the two of you.

SYLVIA: The lies of my bone-idle teenage daughter aren't things I feel the need to be ashamed of. – Speaking of my daughter's vivid imagination, she did come out with a few corkers in her time.

YVONNE: Did she?

SYLVIA: She once told me that Julie Peterson, a girl who lived down the street from us when Yvonne was a little girl. Well, she told me that Julie gave all of her barbie dolls a haircut…

YVONNE: She did.

SYLVIA: But my Yvonne was keen to be a hairdresser when she was older. I just knew she was lying, so you know what I did to her?

YVONNE: Marched her into the upstairs bathroom and gave her a horrible haircut to match the doll's hair?

SYLVIA: How did you know that?

YVONNE: Lucky guess.

SYLVIA: My Yvonne, she always was a daddy's girl. She would have preferred me to have died, instead of him. Silly cow didn't even realise that she helped to put him in the bloody coffin. – Used to steal out of my purse, get on the number sixty bus down to the shops and then she'd reappear half an hour later with six cans of lager. The cheap stuff mind – forty-six pence a can. And she handed them straight to her alcoholic father. The first time I caught her doing it was in April. My Jimmy was dead come August.

YVONNE: Maybe she just thought she was helping him. Are you sure that's how it all happened?

SYLVIA: I swear by almighty God.

(A pause.)

SYLVIA: Loo. I need to use the loo. Have you got a toilet that I can use?

YVONNE: Second door on the left.

(SYLVIA exits. YVONNE waits a moment and then goes into SYLVIA's handbag.)

SYLVIA: *(Off-stage.)* On the left?

YVONNE: That's right. Why don't I make you something to eat? How about a lovely sausage roll?

SYLVIA: *(Off-stage.)* That'd be nice.

(YVONNE pulls out a letter. PHILLIP enters.)

YVONNE: What you doing back?

PHILLIP: Forgot my wallet and Pat won't give me a bacon sandwich on tick. Not lost your touch there, Yvonne! As soon as Fruit Loops is out of the room, you're dipping her purse. Quality.

YVONNE: Be quiet! Here, look at this.

PHILLIP: A letter isn't very exciting, Yvonne. Where's your espionage spirit? – Check the old bag's purse. I bet there's a twenty note in there.

YVONNE: No, look. I was right. There's something wrong with her.

(YVONNE thrusts the letter into PHILLIP's hands, he starts reading the letter. YVONNE takes a sausage roll from the fridge and puts it in the microwave.)

PHILLIP: 'Ms. Sylvia Beveridge.' – Listen, love. I can't be arsed with all of this.

YVONNE: Keep reading!

PHILLIP: 'Blah, blah, blah – diagnosis confirmed; blah, blah, blah – dementia. Blah, blah, blah. Prone to forgetful episodes.' Dementia?

YVONNE: That's what it says! It all makes sense; she's threatened to have my dad come and set about me three times.

PHILLIP: Your Da?

YVONNE: So she said.

PHILLIP: So, Looney Tunes thinks she's back in the 1980's?

YVONNE: Don't call her that!

PHILLIP: After all these years of calling her Daffy Duck and Looney Tunes? And now that she is actually looney, you want me to stop?

YVONNE: PHILLIP!

PHILLIP: I see she brought baggage with her. – Mental and physical.

YVONNE: Listen, I know what she's like better than anyone and she's not okay.

PHILLIP: She's faking it. That letter. It's a cracking forgery.

YVONNE: Why would she be taking the mick?

PHILLIP: Well, it's what she does isn't it? Manipulation.

YVONNE: Phillip!

PHILLIP: Come on, Yvonne! You know what she's like; remember when you were eighteen and she had that 'medical emergency', and you drove all the way to Plymouth and when you got there, she told you that her goldfish had drowned. Come on, how the fuck does a goldfish drown?

YVONNE: She just wanted the company.

PHILLIP: So why didn't she just say that? Instead of having you worrying for six and a half hours?

YVONNE: Because she knew I wouldn't come.

PHILLIP: Why wouldn't you go, Yvonne? I'll tell you why, shall I? It's because she's never really been a proper mum to you, has she? She sat by and let her bloke touch you. – Listen Yvonne, if you want to stand by while she lies about a proper, serious illness – then you can do that. But I'll have no part in it. I'm telling you – I'll play no part in Looney Tunes' games. But don't worry. I'll be there to pick up the pieces.

YVONNE: I know.

(PHILLIP kisses YVONNE on the cheek and exits. SYLVIA enters, back to being her usual self. YVONNE tries to hide the letter.)

YVONNE: You alright.

SYLVIA: Have you been going through my things?

YVONNE: I was just…

SYLVIA: That letter in your hand is my private correspondence! Stealing will do nothing but get you your fingers chopped off.

YVONNE: I wasn't stealing.

SYLVIA: No, you just decided to go through my personal property.

YVONNE: Sylvia, this letter…

SYLVIA: Sylvia? I am your mother.

YVONNE: This letter says that you have dementia.

SYLVIA: That letter is nothing more than a mistake, the doctor even said so himself. – Over the telephone.

YVONNE: Doctors don't make mistakes when it comes to things like this. I'll just phone the surgery.

SYLVIA: You'll do no such thing. They won't tell you anything anyway. It's that new data protection shit.

YVONNE: Of course, they will tell me; I'm your next of kin.

SYLVIA: No, you're not.

YVONNE: What do you mean, "no, you're not"? You've got no one else.

SYLVIA: My sister.

YVONNE: Aunty June? You haven't spoke to her since the seventies. – Aunty Fucking June?

SYLVIA: Who do you think I've been living with?

YVONNE: You could've come to me.

SYLVIA: Because you'd have done the world of good, wouldn't you? – Not exactly a palace you live in, is it?

YVONNE: Happy family, happy home.

SYLVIA: Bullshit, Yvonne.

YVONNE: No, it's not a Palace – but its home.

SYLVIA: Some home.

YVONNE: Home, mother. For eighteen years. Over there, near the washing machine. That's where Lip took his first steps. In the bath upstairs – that's where he said his first word. It might have been 'dad' but still – this house is mine. All mine. And Phillip's, and Lip's.

SYLVIA: That's a load of shite, Yvonne. And you know it.

YVONNE: Why did you come here? – Just to torture me? Or because you had nowhere else to go?

SYLVIA: You know, every once in a while, every girl needs their mummy to come and give them – give them a reality check.

YVONNE: A reality check?

SYLVIA: The way you let your young lad speak to you. It's just unacceptable.

YVONNE: He's a teenager. He's going through the motions.

SYLVIA: Well, you want to reign it in… I should've reigned you in when I had the chance. Maybe, if I did, my life – my relationship with you would be different. Different for the better.

(A pause.)

YVONNE: Can we talk about this letter from your doctor?

SYLVIA: I told you. It's a mistake. Nothing more than that.

YVONNE: They don't tell you that you've got this if you don't. This is serious.

SYLVIA: Listen, I haven't got dementia. Difficulty carrying out daily activities. I got here, didn't I? Impaired judgement? I still know your husband's a wanker. Impaired language skills? I don't have any of that.

YVONNE: Done your research, have you? What about memory loss?

SYLVIA: Well, who isn't a bit forgetful sometimes?

YVONNE: Can I ask you some questions? What's your name?

SYLVIA: Sylvia Beveridge. How incapable do you think I am?

YVONNE: Where are you from?

SYLVIA: Fucking hell, it's like playing 'Who Wants to Be a Millionaire.' – Plymouth. Final answer.

(There's a change in SYLVIA. *She starts humming a tune.)*

YVONNE: Mother! I am trying to talk to you.

(A timer goes off. YVONNE *turns away to sort the timer.)*

YVONNE: And I am trying to make you something to eat!

*(*YVONNE *puts the sausage roll on the plate.* SYLVIA *stands up and walks over to* YVONNE, *who is still standing with her back to* SYLVIA.*)*

SYLVIA: Don't you turn your back on me!

YVONNE: I'm not. I'm just trying to make you something to eat!

SYLVIA: ALWAYS HAD TO HAVE THE LAST WORD, DIDN'T YOU? *(SYLVIA takes the plate from YVONNE and throws it onto the kitchen floor.)* How many times have I told you about that mouth of yours? You gobby little cow! When you're under my roof you do as I say, alright?

YVONNE: Mum…

(There is a change in SYLVIA.)

SYLVIA: Do you think I could see my room, please.

YVONNE: Yes. I'll show you.

(The two stand up and go to walk to LIP's bedroom.)

SYLVIA: Can you grab my cases for me please. – Yvonne.

YVONNE: Yeah.

(YVONNE grabs the cases and the two go to exit.)

SYLVIA: My handbag.

(SYLVIA retrieves her handbag.)

YVONNE: This way…

SYLVIA: And I'd appreciate it if you could give me my doctor's letter back. Need to clean that mess up as well.

YVONNE: Of course.

(The two exit. Blackout. As the lights come back up, the stage curtains have been closed. PHILLIP *and* LIP *enter in front of the curtains, they're in the street.)*

LIP: Where you going?

PHILLIP: I don't know son, get a bacon roll or something as long as I'm away from her.

LIP: I don't understand why my grandma is stopping with us.

PHILLIP: Cause your mother is soft, son. Can't say no to the old bat.

LIP: Fair enough.

PHILLIP: Now, you've got your mum worried sick that you're going to run off to the army.

LIP: I'm thinking about it.

PHILLIP: Don't be an idiot, son. You wouldn't last five minutes in the army. Me and you, we're different kinds of men. We know our place. We're meant to stay within our confines. Whoever up there decided that we should live in this shithole decided that for a reason. – Fighting for Queen and Country isn't everything it's cracked up to be.

LIP: I'm sick of seeing the same things day after day.

PHILLIP: Well, get on the bus and go to London for the weekend.

LIP: That's not what I'm talking about.

PHILLIP: You don't need to be getting these grand ideas about jetting off to the desert to fight the fucking Taliban. Come on, son. Think about it, you've got a good job. Do you really want to throw all of that away?

LIP: I work in a corner shop.

PHILLIP: And Katrina did your mum a favour giving you that job. – Don't let me down Lip.

(PHILLIP slaps LIP on the back and walks off.)

LIP: You not gonna buy me breakfast?

PHILLIP: You know where the cafe is.

(LIP huffs and exits. PHILLIP makes sure he is long gone before he pulls out his mobile and dials a number.)

PHILLIP: Alright, Nicky? – It's Phillip. Do you still want me to come over today? – Just down on the corner of Westerhouse Road. – Decent. And I wanted to make sure – you definitely want me to be naked, don't you? – Right, okay. See you in a bit.

(PHILLIP exits. Blackout.)

Scene Two
Sunday. 8PM. The Back Door.

(PHILLIP is sitting on the edge of the stage, as if he's leaning against the back door of the house.)

PHILLIP: You think you've had a shite day? Take a look at my life. Just when I think I've got it all, that old cow shows up on my doorstep. MY fucking doorstep. She swans in here with a sick note and a suitcase and Yvonne offers her a bed and a cuppa. I wouldn't piss on the old bat if she was burning. What is it the bible says? "You don't socialise with wicked or invite Evil as your houseguest." Well Yvonne, you've really told God to go fuck himself on that one. That's all this is. Just one giant fucking headache. She's only been here for about eight hours and this is what I'm reduced to. Hiding in away in my room like fucking Rapunzel in her tower so I don't have listen to her bullshit excuses as to why she's a shite mother. A shite person. Did you know she's having another one? More milk, less cans. I AM LIVING THE DREAM, BOYS! *(PHILLIP is silent for a while and he appears to have fallen asleep. He suddenly sits up again.)* They're going to see it all. Manhood and all sorts. All of them. Just– looking at me. Standing there, bollock naked whilst they soak it all in. *(He laughs.)* Do you like what you see do you?

(Instant blackout.)

Scene Three
Sunday. 10PM. The Kitchen.

*(*LIP *enters holding a hoodie.* YVONNE *is sitting at the kitchen table reading* SYLVIA's *diary.)*

LIP: I didn't know if you'd still be up.

YVONNE: Just trying to figure out what to do about your grandma.

LIP: You don't want to stress too much. You hear all the time about stress causing birds to go into labour.

YVONNE: 'Birds'? *Lovely.*

LIP: You know what I mean. So, where am I sleeping?

YVONNE: Sofa.

LIP: How long for Mam?

YVONNE: Just a couple of nights.

LIP: Why's she even here?

YVONNE: She's come to see you, for your eighteenth.

LIP: That was two weeks ago.

YVONNE: She never was one for turning up on time.

LIP: So why is she really here?

YVONNE: (*She snaps.*) I don't know Lip!

LIP: Jesus. Sorry I asked.

(*LIP turns to exit.*)

YVONNE: Wait, Lip. I'm sorry. Listen, I don't know why she's really here but she's not well and regardless of what your father says or thinks, I want to help her. Well, wanting to is something else but she needs my help. All of our help.

LIP: Why doesn't dad want to help?

YVONNE: That's a long story son.

LIP: Fair enough.

(*A pause.*)

LIP: Do you think you'll be able to get this stain out?

YVONNE: Let's see it.

(*LIP hands over the hoodie.*)

LIP: I had a jam doughnut out of Greggs after football.

YVONNE: And you slopped it all down yourself? – Your Mam always knows, Phillip.

LIP: What's with you 'full-naming' me?

YVONNE: I nearly forgot to ask; have we fell out?

LIP: What do you mean?

YVONNE: You haven't agreed to be my friend.

LIP: What're you talking about?

YVONNE: Facebook.

LIP: Don't start this again…

YVONNE: Did you see Danny Taylor got sentenced at the weekend? – Big Mandy shared a post all about it on Facebook.

LIP: I know.

YVONNE: Four years.

LIP: Mental.

YVONNE: Well, that's what you get for getting involved in drugs. – You aren't doing drugs, are you?

LIP: No.

YVONNE: It's more common than you think. Chinese Claire from my 'mummy and baby' classes shared a video on Facebook last week from one of those online documentaries, and they said on there, that around here it is easier and quicker to get cocaine delivered to you than it is to get a pizza delivered.

LIP: Every lad and their dog deals it around here.

(YVONNE pretends that she didn't hear that.)

YVONNE: You know, they even said that – on average, a gram of cocaine is cheaper than a pair of Air Max. Absolute madness, I tell ya.

LIP: That's bullshit, a gram is... So, do you think that you'll get that stain out?

YVONNE: I'll try.

(Blackout.)

Scene Four
Monday. 10AM. The Kitchen.

(PHILLIP is sitting at the table counting pennies from a jar labelled 'Lip's Car Fund' and drinking occasionally from a can of lager. LIP enters the kitchen, which prompts PHILLIP to quickly hide the jar.)

LIP: *(Off-stage.)* MAM! MAM?

(LIP enters.)

PHILLIP: Alright, son?

LIP: Alright.

(LIP grabs a packet of crisps.)

PHILLIP: You doing much today?

LIP: Not really. Where's the bread?

PHILLIP: Next doors had it.

LIP: Course. – The cereal?

PHILLIP: Daffy Duck had the last of it.

LIP: Well, can I have one of your cans?

PHILLIP: No.

LIP: Why?

PHILLIP: It's early in the day. Just because you're not at work, that doesn't mean you can sit around the house all day drinking.

LIP: You do it!

PHILLIP: Son, I am a valuable member of our community. I have worked hard for all these years; I am entitled to do whatever I like.

(LIP laughs.)

LIP: You've never worked a day in your life. – Whatever. Since when did you turn into a sensible parent?

PHILLIP: Lip. Son. I'm not refusing you a can to win 'parent of the year', I've got three cans left. One. Two. Three. Three left and my dole money doesn't come in until tomorrow and no one will give me anything on tick. So, no. You can't have one; because they're mine.

LIP: Oh yeah. And you need those for when you're doing fuck all but sitting around the house all day drinking.

PHILLIP: Precisely. Get your own. *(Pause.)* You seeing any of your girlfriends today, Casanova?

LIP: What's it to you?

PHILLIP: It's just a question, son. – What are their names again? Rosie and Annie?

LIP: Anna.

PHILLIP: Right enough. It's hard enough keeping up with you and your two girlfriends.

LIP: I haven't got two girlfriends! They're just – nothing. – And anyway, since when did you decide to take an interest in my life?

PHILLIP: That's a bit harsh, son. But alright, I'll leave you be. Actually, your girlfriends are my business when you're back and forth, bouncing up and down on that bloody bed at four in the morning.

LIP: DAD!

PHILLIP: Okay! I'm sorry. I'll shut up. Just gonna do me a favour? Gag them so they're not so noisy next time.

LIP: Fucks sake, Dad! Shut up!

PHILLIP: Right! That's me finished. I've had my fun. I'll leave it at that. Christ, God forbid your old man try and have a bit of a laugh with you. When did you become such a prick?

(There is a knock at the door, RHONDA *enters.)*

RHONDA: Hello! Only me.

PHILLIP: Here we go…

LIP: Alright?

PHILLIP: Alright, Rhonda?

RHONDA: Alright Phil. Is Yvonne in?

LIP: No, she's away up to the shops.

RHONDA: Do you think I could be a pest and borrow that salt and pepper? I've just made soup for Gary's lunch, and he said that it's tasteless. Can you believe that? Honestly, I've had it up to here with the man.

(She points to the bottles of salt and pepper on the table.)

PHILLIP: Aye.

RHONDA: Thanks.

LIP: No bother.

RHONDA: Absolute life savers, I'm telling you.

(PHILLIP ushers RHONDA out.)

PHILLIP: Local heroes, I know. I'll tell Yvonne you were looking for her.

RHONDA: Thanks, love.

PHILLIP: Bye Rhonda.

(RHONDA exits.)

PHILLIP: Bye, bye now!

LIP: That's the fifth Rhonda raid this week.

PHILLIP: The woman's a bloody nightmare.

LIP: Tell me about it.

PHILLIP: I need to go out. If she comes back, don't give her anything.

LIP: Right.

(PHILLIP picks up his phone and dials Yvonne.)

PHILLIP: Hello? Yvonne, love. – You need to bring back some salt and pepper. – I know we did, Rhonda's had it.

(PHILLIP exits. LIP's phone rings. He answers it.)

LIP: Alright Ben? Yeah, I'm up for it. - Right no bother, I'm just gonna grab something to eat and then I'll be out, just pick me up outside mine.

(LIP opens the fridge and pulls out a dildo. He throws it back in.)

LIP: Kinky bastards.

(Blackout.)

Scene Five
Monday. 12PM. The Kitchen.

(YVONNE is sitting at the kitchen table with a cup of tea and there are papers all over the table. RHONDA knocks and then enters. She is carrying a gift bag.)

RHONDA: Hello Yvonne love.

YVONNE: Hi Rhonda. Kettle's just boiled.

RHONDA: Grand.

(RHONDA, who clearly knows her way around the kitchen, sets her bag down and makes herself a cup of tea. YVONNE swallows a tablet.)

YVONNE: What have you got for me today?

RHONDA: Just you wait. I think you'll be pleased.

YVONNE: I'm sure I will be.

RHONDA: Pork Pie Pat came and picked hers up last night and my phones not stopped buzzing all morning with her good reviews.

YVONNE: I bet she's not stopped buzzing since last night.

RHONDA: Honestly, the new stuff they're coming out with. It's unbelievable.

YVONNE: I meant to say, have you read this book?

(YVONNE pulls out a copy of 'Fifty Shades of Grey' from her handbag.)

RHONDA: I read that last year, when it first came out. All three of them. Catch up.

YVONNE: I saw the film not long ago, didn't know it was a book. Pat turned me onto it.

RHONDA: Of course, she did, she loves a bit of erotica. You know the only reason the woman bought a kindle was because she could make it vibrate. – Dirty bitch.

(They both laugh.)

RHONDA: What we like? Here, have a look.

(RHONDA passes the bag to YVONNE.)

YVONNE: Some haul this month. I can't wait to get some alone time. With any luck Phillip will do his usual and stay in the Fox and Hound until early hours.

RHONDA: You not wanting to get him involved?

(They both laugh hysterically.)

YVONNE: Not tonight love, tonight's for me. I'm in need of some T.L.C and this will definitely do the trick.

RHONDA: Right you are. Got paid last week so treated myself to the Rampant G Pro, you know the one I mean?

RHONDA & YVONNE: *(They both hold up two fingers.)* With the fingers.

YVONNE: You'll need to let me know how it is, maybe next month I'll treat myself. I'll double up Lip's rent money and go all out.

RHONDA: Hey that's not a bad idea that. If you're looking for a review, I can let you read the texts I got from Pork Pie Pat.

YVONNE: No thanks. I don't want to be completely put off.

RHONDA: You're right.

YVONNE: It's her husband I feel sorry for. Imagine coming up against Pork Pie Pat swinging six inches of rubber and rotating metal balls.

RHONDA & YVONNE: Poor Simon.

YVONNE: The man walks like John Wayne. Bless her. Tell you what though, I bet she's good for business.

RHONDA: Too right. Pork Pie Pat's helping pay off the car insurance.

YVONNE: Well, there you go, cheers to Pat and all her toys.

(They both clink cups, in a 'cheers'. Rhonda's phone vibrates.)

RHONDA: Right, I'll have to shoot, that's Katrina, she's after her order.

(YVONNE *swallows another tablet.*)

RHONDA: Christ Yvonne, those aren't smarties you know.

YVONNE: Can't shift this heartburn. Been in agony all night.

RHONDA: That means you're having a girl. The more hair the babies got on her head, the worse the burn.

YVONNE: So, I've heard. It's either that or the extra stress that just turned up.

RHONDA: Your mam? What's wrong?

YVONNE: It's nothing.

RHONDA: Come on Yvonne love, a problem shared is a problem halved. If you can't tell your best friend, then who can you tell?

YVONNE: You watch too much Loose Women.

RHONDA: Yes, but I'm much better looking than Andrea McClean.

YVONNE: And you've got bigger tits. – I'm worried about her. And then I feel guilty for worrying about her. Then I feel guilty for feeling guilty.

RHONDA: Right…

YVONNE: I know that makes no sense. I've spent so much of my life resenting her. And not to mention that when she was around, she was useless. But now she's here and she's got dementia and she's probably scared. Even though she doesn't show it. I hated her so much, but I never wanted something like this to happen.

RHONDA: I don't think you really hated her. I think maybe you were just angry. The two can feel very similar.

YVONNE: Maybe. I want her to be okay and of course I'm going to help but she's just swanned in here and dug up a lot of memories that I'd managed to lock away.

RHONDA: Well, that's never good for ya. Any Doctor will tell you that.

YVONNE: I know. I pushed all that away so I could focus on bringing up Lip and I got used to her never being around. And now I've got a new baby to look after as well as my mother. It feels like a lot all at once, ya know?

RHONDA: You're a bloody saint Yvonne. Listen, it's normal to feel a bit overwhelmed by it all. She took you by surprise and any normal person in your position would feel just as flustered. Have you tried speaking to her?

YVONNE: A little bit, but it's hard. One minute, she's there speaking as normal and the next minute she thinks I'm a kid. In both scenarios she's always right and I'm the bad guy. She's so stubborn.

(RHONDA looks at the papers.)

RHONDA: What's all this?

YVONNE: Dementia. Advice, stories. I don't really know Rhonda.

RHONDA: Come on now, there's no use filling yourself full of these.

YVONNE: I'm in over me head Rhond. I've got no clue what I'm doing.

RHONDA: None of us do.

YVONNE: There's so much involved Rhond. So much care. Round the clock attention. I don't know if I can give her that.

RHONDA: Stick her in a care home.

YVONNE: She's me Mam. I can't do that to her. – And I've looked. They cost thousands, and I can't afford that, not with another baby coming.

RHONDA: Phone your brother.

YVONNE: Mark cares less than I do.

RHONDA: He's just as responsible for her as you are.

YVONNE: Mark's never been responsible.

RHONDA: Well, we can have a whip round.

YVONNE: No. I'm not a charity case.

RHONDA: We can get some funding. Our Lisa's a nurse. She'll know something.

YVONNE: Why did she have to come, Rhonda? I haven't seen her in years, since before Lip was born. Couldn't she just have stayed in Plymouth. Let me Aunty June phone me in a couple month time and tell me that I needed to dig out me funeral hat.

RHONDA: Yvonne. She's your mam.

YVONNE: You don't know her Rhonda, not like I do.

RHONDA: It doesn't matter.

YVONNE: She's always been the same. Never had a thought about anyone else, always looking after number one. And now she's still doing the same and half the time she doesn't know her arse from her elbow.

RHONDA: You need to calm down. You're gonna do yourself in.

YVONNE: What am I gonna do Rhonda? Look at this one, this woman's Mam; she kept going missing. Fourteen times they found her, wandering the streets of Liverpool in a dressing gown and nightie. I don't want that for me Mam. She's not that type of woman. She's always been strong. Done everything on her own terms for the most part, and now she's gonna go out doing what she does best, sucking the fucking joy out of everything.

RHONDA: Yvonne you can't…

YVONNE: One winter, it was proper cold, and I remember sitting by the window with me Mam. We were watching me neighbour, he was pulling massive icicles off his house, off the gutters. And I asked her why he was doing it. She said they could fall off and stab someone if they got too heavy and with any luck ours would get big enough and my dad would walk under one.

RHONDA: Jesus.

YVONNE: I was nine. Maybe ten. As soon as she fucked off down the bingo, I got the mop and went round the house, I made sure all of the icicles were gone. She came back that night, I pretended to be asleep and she just stood in me door, laughing.

(There is a pause. YVONNE *looks deep in thought then turns to* RHONDA.*)*

YVONNE: I'll figure it out. I'm ok really. Just having one of those days. You better get going. I wouldn't like to see Katrina angry and horny.

RHONDA: Christ no, can't be having that can we? Right you are, I better be off.

YVONNE: Alright Rhonda, thanks for dropping that off, you've made my night.

RHONDA: Pleasure doing business with you.

YVONNE: I can assure you; the pleasure will be all mine.

RHONDA: Let me know how it goes.

YVONNE: Thanks Rhonda, I really appreciate it. Before you go let me just go and get that money that I owe you. I left it in my bedside table so I wouldn't spend it.

(YVONNE goes off to the bedroom. RHONDA notices a box full of junk on the kitchen floor and begins to rummage through it. She picks up and examines various different items.)

YVONNE: Sorry love, I can't find that money anywhere, no doubt Phillip's nicked it and gone down the pub. I'll give it to you on Tuesday.

RHONDA: That's no bother. What's this box?

YVONNE: Charity shop junk that Phillip's been hoarding in the cupboard under the stairs. Needed to sort a space out for the baby's cot.

(RHONDA pulls a commemorative plate from Charles and Diana's Wedding from the box of junk.)

RHONDA: Do you mind if I borrow this commemorative plate from Charles and Diana's wedding from nineteen-eighty-one? My mam loved Diana and I would love to show her this.

YVONNE: Sure, take whatever you want. Out of the box.

RHONDA: Oh thanks, Yvonne. You've made my day.

YVONNE: Well, hopefully you've just made my night.

RHONDA: Cheers love. Right, I better be off, plenty more people to please.

YVONNE: Bye.

RHONDA: See you later. And remember, I'm just next door if you ever need to chat. *(A pause.)* Thanks for the plate.

(RHONDA exits.)

YVONNE: And the rest.

(RHONDA re-enters.)

RHONDA: Did you say something, love?

(YVONNE raises her mug to RHONDA.)

YVONNE: You're the best!

(YVONNE takes another look in the box before opening 'Fifty Shades of Grey' again. A huge smile appears on her face. LIP enters.)

LIP: Have you seen my ball?

YVONNE: It's in your bedroom.

LIP: Alright.

YVONNE: Where you going?

LIP: Just out in the garden. I think Ben's going to come over. But I need to talk to you about something. *(LIP notices the bag.)* What's that?

YVONNE: My order off of Rhonda.

*(*YVONNE *takes the bag off of the table.)*

LIP: A bag of dildos on our kitchen table? Lovely.

YVONNE: That reminds me; have you been shaving your downstairs bits in the bathroom? Because it's really not nice having to clean up in there after you've done that.

LIP: What? No.

YVONNE: Listen, there's no shame in shaving your bits, just clean it up after.

LIP: Mam…

YVONNE: Me and your grandma use that bath and I'm sick of sitting in your hairs.

LIP: Listen, I don't shave my pubes.

YVONNE: Well, who is it? Your father keeps a full bush, I can't reach, and I highly doubt your grandma is up there trimming her lady garden.

LIP: Don't ever talk to me about my grandma's minge. It's not fucking me.

(The stage lights go down on YVONNE *and come up on* LIP, *who is standing down stage centre.)*

LIP: The one thing that teachers always used to say to me was: "Phillip, you're never going to do anything with your life." Because that was one of the only things I was good at in school. Doing nothing. Unless you count being a nuisance or generally just causing trouble. And now, I'm proving them right. What am I doing? Working in a fucking corner shop for pennies, that's what. So, everyone just thought that I'd turn into my dad. In name and nature. Just some alcoholic roaming the streets looking for someone to buy me a pint. And this, *(LIP produces an envelope.)* was my chance to do something good and not become a carbon copy of my dad. How good would I look, coming back here in an army uniform? And then when I saw those teachers, and they'd be like: "Hello Phillip! What are you doing with yourself now?" and I would say, "FIGHTING IN FUCKING WARS TO KEEP YOUR ARSE SAFE." That would feel good. Throwing a middle finger up to the old fuckers. But no. *(LIP pulls the letter out of the envelope.)* 'Dear Phillip. After careful consideration, we have decided not to progress with your application due to an unsatisfactory medical examination. Thank you for your interest in The British Army and we wish you the best of luck with your future endeavours. Yours, Samuel Duff. Recruitment.'…RECRUITMENT? Asthma. And not just asthma. Really fucking bad asthma. But how does that affect me patrolling the perimeter of some town on the edge of a jungle, and in a split second; drop to the floor, rifle in hand. Ready to take that shot. – I could do that. I never thought that it would be 'I was born in Bricklethwaite, but I was made in the British Army.' I just thought it might've been my turn to find something I was good at, you know. Something that was mine.

(Blackout.)

Scene Six
Monday. 2PM. The Kitchen.

*(*SYLVIA *is dancing around the kitchen, emptying the contents of* YVONNE's *shopping bag. She's blowing condoms up like they're balloons.)*

SYLVIA: *"Voulez-vous! AHA! (Double blow into the condom.) Take it now or leave it! AHA! (Double blow into the condom.)…"*

*(*RHONDA *enters.)*

RHONDA: Alright Sylvia, love? It's me, Rhonda. From next door.

SYLVIA: I know. *The Dog Lady.*

RHONDA: Well, I've been called worse. – Anyway, I've just popped over to borrow some toothpaste. Is Yvonne in?

SYLVIA: No, she's not. And don't phone her. This is all supposed to be a surprise.

*(*RHONDA *looks around the room, she is puzzled.)*

RHONDA: What is?

SYLVIA: *The party.* I'm throwing her a surprise birthday party.

RHONDA: Oooh! I love a party! Is it just family, or are friends welcome too?

SYLVIA: Of course, acquaintances are welcome! You can come, darling. Bring your husband too. – Starts at four.

(RHONDA *doesn't like that* SYLVIA *has downgraded her to 'an acquaintance'.*)

RHONDA: Oh, yes! How exciting? I better get home and get my glad rags on.

SYLVIA: Great, I'll see you at four.

RHONDA: I'm just going to grab that toothpaste.

SYLVIA: Here, love. Yvonne bought a fresh tube today. You take that one.

(SYLVIA *hands* RHONDA *a tube of toothpaste from* YVONNE's *shopping bag.*)

RHONDA: Thanks, Sylvia. (RHONDA *laughs as she picks the condoms up off the table.*) I think it's a bit too late for Yvonne to start using these.

SYLVIA: Right. Yes.

(SYLVIA *takes the condoms from* RHONDA *and turns them in her hands.*)

RHONDA: Right, Sylvia, my love. I'll see you at four for the *'partay'!* Let me know if you need any help getting set up.

SYLVIA: See you then, dear.

(RHONDA *exits with the toothpaste.* SYLVIA *goes over to the CD player and turns the music up; "Dancing Queen" is playing. She pulls a black bag out from under the table that is filled with blown up condoms. She empties them all over the floor and she starts blowing more condoms up and singing in between blows.* YVONNE *enters.)*

SYLVIA: *"Dancing Queen, feel the beat of the tangerine. OH YEAH! YOU CAN DANCE…"*

YVONNE: …Mam!

(YVONNE *storms over to the CD player and turns it off.)*

SYLVIA: *"YOU CAN DANCE, YOU CAN JIVE. HAVING THE TIME OF YOUR LIFE!"* – I was listening to that!

YVONNE: Yeah, and meanwhile, the whole Estate is deaf.

SYLVIA: That song is a classic. I don't think anyone will mind, especially her next door who falls asleep to the sound of fourteen bulldogs snoring.

(YVONNE *notices the blown-up condoms that are scattered all over the floor.)*

YVONNE: What are you doing?

SYLVIA I was dancing to a classic.

YVONNE: Not that! Those. And that.

(YVONNE *points to the un-inflated condom in* SYLVIA's *hand.)*

SYLVIA: It's for the party. I'm making a real effort this year.

YVONNE: What party?

SYLVIA: Yvonne's birthday party. She's turning seventeen, and she's always wanted a big party, one of those – what's it called? A sweet seventeenth. Although if I'm being honest there's nothing sweet about being seventeen, it's all sneaking around, drinking in parks and shagging anything that moves.

YVONNE: …that's enough mother. In fact, that's WAY too much.

SYLVIA: Prude. I found these in that bag, so I thought I'd decorate for the party; all I'm missing is a banner to go over there. You're here now love, fancy running down the shop for a banner?

YVONNE: There's condoms all over the floor, I don't think a banner is going to help turn this place into a party bonanza.

(SYLVIA ignores YVONNE.)

SYLVIA: Pink if they've got it and preferably saying "Happy Seventeenth Birthday." Oh, and a cake, I haven't got a cake yet. Any kind will do she's not fussy when it comes to food, probably why she's getting a bit fat.

YVONNE: Well, that's just lovely. Mam – Sylvia there's no party. It's me Yvonne, I'm not Seventeen anymore; I'm thirty-eight, and it's not even my birthday, and I really don't need a party, okay? The thought is lovely, thank you, but I don't need a party and I certainly don't need twenty ribbed balloons floating around my kitchen. – And I was never fat!

*(*PHILLIP *enters.)*

PHILLIP: Hello love. Alright Sylvia.

SYLVIA: Phillip…

*(*PHILLIP *pulls out a beer from the fridge and takes a swig. He notices his surroundings and nearly chokes.)*

PHILLIP: Jesus Christ, what the Hell is going on here?

SYLVIA: I'm trying to throw my daughter a party.

YVONNE: For the last time we are not having a party and your daughter, is standing right here. Maybe you should go for a little lie down, Mam. Rest for a bit, wouldn't you like to do that?

SYLVIA: I don't need a lie down! I'm not ancient or incompetent. What I need is for you to run down to the shop and pick up a banner and a cake.

YVONNE: Phillip, will you please tell her that we are not having a party.

SYLVIA: Yeah, good luck getting the alcoholic to turn down a party.

YVONNE: Mam!

PHILLIP: This looks more like one of them Ann Summers parties you like to go to.

(LIP *enters and notices the condoms straight away.*)

PHILLIP: Alright son?

LIP: What is wrong with everyone in this house?

SYLVIA: Come and help me blow up some balloons, will you? They keep slipping out me hands.

LIP: Why the fuck is my grandma playing with condoms?

SYLVIA: It's a party.

YVONNE: For Christ's sake.

LIP: What is wrong with everyone in this house?

PHILLIP: I've been trying to figure that one out for years.

LIP: I thought you weren't buying me condoms.

PHILLIP: You bought these? For the bed breaker?

LIP: Dad!

YVONNE: I wasn't going to. But I just don't want you to find yourself short, when you're you know – doing it.

LIP: Right, well thank you for that. But I won't be doing it ever again because I am going to my bedroom to kill myself.

(LIP turns and exits quickly.)

PHILLIP: Yeah, I best be off too, I was busy upstairs.

YVONNE: You were only watching Richard and Judy! You're not going anywhere.

SYLVIA: So, my Vonnie's sweet seventeenth?

YVONNE: Fine! Throw the bloody party but no banners. And no fucking condoms!

SYLVIA: Great, just you wait and see how excited Yvonne will be. Just make sure all birthday cards go to me first, I want to see how much I've pulled in this year. Be on the lookout for the pink envelopes with the fancy writing, those are from her Aunty June and she always puts in a fifty.

(YVONNE exits.)

YVONNE: *(As she exits.)* Unbelievable. *(Off-stage.)* And by the way a tangerine is an Orange! FEEL – THE – BEAT – OF – THE – TAMBORINE.

(PHILLIP shouts to YVONNE.)

PHILLIP: You bought him the condoms, so you're buying him the next bed!

YVONNE: *(Off-stage)* FUCK OFF!

PHILLIP: Right, well I better go get ready for this party.

SYLVIA: Party starts at four!

(PHILLIP grabs the remaining cans from the fridge and exits. SYLVIA picks up another condom and starts blowing it up.)

SYLVIA: Oooh! Sherbet!

(Blackout.)

Scene Seven
Monday. 4PM. The Kitchen and the Living Room.

*(*YVONNE, LIP *(who is wearing a football strip), and* PHILLIP *are sitting around the kitchen table. They are waiting for* SYLVIA *to start the party.)*

LIP: How long do I have to stay here for?

YVONNE: I told you, all night! – We haven't had a family night in God knows how long!

PHILLIP: I wonder why?

YVONNE: Shut up and let her throw the stupid party. It might help her with whatever's going on upstairs!

LIP: I've got a life, you know!

YVONNE: Phil, will you have a word with him?

PHILLIP: Listen, son. We're only doing this to humour your Gran. All I'm saying is give it half an hour and you'll be out of here! And you know what your mother is like when she's had a few drinks, she'll let you do whatever you want.

YVONNE: PHIL! I'm only having one or two drinks. Got the baby to think about.

LIP: Why not get pissed then? Because we all know you haven't stopped smoking.

PHILLIP: Here, son.

(PHILLIP *hands* LIP *a can of beer.*)

LIP: Cheers.

PHILLIP: I'm with you on this one. I want this to be over as soon as possible.

(RHONDA *enters.*)

RHONDA: Hello lovelies! Are we ready for a good, old-fashioned night in the house?

PHILLIP: Absolutely. *(To* LIP.*)* Put a padlock on the fridge.

YVONNE: Where's Gary?

RHONDA: He sends his apologies. One of the charity lads phoned and he's had to jump into replace one of the boys in this month's sponsored event. He's doing a sponsored singathon to Songs of Praise for all the sex addicts in the local area.

PHILLIP: How lovely.

YVONNE: It's good that you could come though.

PHILLIP: Thank the Heavens!

(YVONNE *nudges* PHILLIP.*)

SYLVIA: *(Off-stage.)* Are you ready for me? – Lip be a good boy and put the music on.

(LIP *turns the music on and 'Every Time We Touch' by Cascada starts playing.* SYLVIA *enters. She is wearing a dress, a tacky, plastic silver crown and a sash that is clearly handmade that reads 'Rear of Year 1982'.)*

SYLVIA: It's not bad, is it? I mean, it's not an exact replica, but it's pretty close to the outfit that I wore when I won the actual title.

RHONDA: What does that sash say?

SYLVIA: "Rear of the Year 1982."

YVONNE: Why are you wearing that?

SYLVIA: I told you, it's a fancy-dress party.

YVONNE: You never told us that.

SYLVIA: I did! I specifically remember telling you. Lip knew, look! He's come as a footballer!

LIP: I dress like this all the time! I didn't know it was fancy-dress.

SYLVIA: I told Rhonda! Look at the dog hairs on her shoulders! She's come as a dog!

LIP: She is a dog breeder!

YVONNE: I'm sorry, Rhonda.

RHONDA: Not to worry, no harm done.

(RHONDA *picks some dog hairs off of her shoulders.*)

SYLVIA: You know, Yvonne. I was thinking earlier, maybe we could plant an apple tree in the garden. You always loved apples when you were younger.

YVONNE: As long as it's a Pink Lady tree.

SYLVIA: I prefer a juicy Cox; I won't lie to you.

LIP: *(Sarcastically.)* I love my life.

RHONDA: Why don't we play a drinking game?

SYLVIA: That's a grand idea! I haven't played a drinking game since the start of the nineties! I think John Major had just been voted into Downing Street the last time I played 'Never Have I Ever'.

RHONDA: That's a good one.

SYLVIA: I'll start! Never have I ever. –

LIP: That's it. I'm away out.

PHILLIP: You finished with that tinny, son?

LIP: Have at it.

(LIP *hands the can of beer to* PHILLIP *and exits.*)

SYLVIA: Never have I ever seen two people naked at the same time.

PHILLIP: I was thinking, maybe I should retire up to the bedroom as well.

(SYLVIA *and* RHONDA *both drink.*)

YVONNE: Don't you move a muscle.

PHILLIP: But Lip left…

YVONNE: I said don't move.

RHONDA: Never have I ever fancied my best mate's son.

(RHONDA *takes a drink. Everyone stares at her. Blackout. The lights come back up and the cast, bar* LIP *are dancing to "House of Fun".*)

END OF ACT ONE

Scene Eight

Tuesday. 12AM. The Kitchen and the Living Room.

(As the lights come back up, PHILLIP *is alone in the kitchen with* RHONDA. YVONNE *and* SYLVIA *are in the living room. Everyone is clearly intoxicated.)*

RHONDA: Well, I should call it a night. Gary should be getting back soon. He's going to go spare. He keeps that Whisky for watching the darts!

PHILLIP: What time is it?

RHONDA: I dunno, midnight.

*(*YVONNE *sits on the armchair in silence. Occasionally drinking from her wine glass.* SYLVIA *is in a dressing gown. She's holding a hairbrush. She's timid here, it's almost as if she's reverted to her younger self.)*

YVONNE: You should be in bed.

SYLVIA: I haven't brushed my hair.

YVONNE: So?

SYLVIA: Can't sleep without brushing me hair. Me mam always said that if you wanted long hair you had to brush it a hundred times.

*(*YVONNE *hesitates.)*

YVONNE: Come here then.

*(*YVONNE *moves and* SYLVIA *sits on the armchair, she hands* YVONNE *the hairbrush and* YVONNE *starts brushing her hair.)*

SYLVIA: I've got a daughter, you know.

YVONNE: Aha.

SYLVIA: I used to brush her hair.

YVONNE: That's nice.

SYLVIA: We used to sit by the fire after she'd had a bath, I'd brush her hair for hours, when she were a proper little girl, five or six I mean. I used to sing to her. Sometimes she'd sing back.

YVONNE: I know…

SYLVIA: I wish I knew where she was.

(There's a long silence as YVONNE *carries on brushing her hair. After a moment she stops.)*

YVONNE: There. All done.

SYLVIA: Would you like me to brush your hair?

*(*YVONNE *is hesitant.)*

YVONNE: Go on then.

(They switch places and SYLVIA *starts brushing* YVONNE'S *hair. There's another silence.* SYLVIA *starts*

65

singing 'A Natural Woman' by Aretha Franklin as she brushes. YVONNE *joins in with the singing halfway through.)*

SYLVIA: *"Lookin' out on the mornin' rain. I used to feel so uninspired. And when I knew I had to face another day, oh it made me feel so tired. Before the day I met you, life was so unkind, but you're the key to my peace of mind. Cause you make me feel, you make me feel, you make me feel like a natural woman."*

*(*YVONNE *sobs. There's a pause.* SYLVIA *seems to remember who she is.)*

SYLVIA: We were like two totally different people tonight. If I were watching the pair of us, I wouldn't have been able to tell that you hate me.

YVONNE: I don't…

SYLVIA: You do, and who can blame you? I've been back with you for such a short time, but I'm realising that for all of those years, all of those years that I sat back and just didn't do anything. I've realised that I was wrong, all that time. I was wrong.

YVONNE: We don't need to talk about this tonight.

SYLVIA: No. You're right. We don't.

(There is a change in SYLVIA.*)*

YVONNE: Everything alright for you?

SYLVIA: Grand. – Are you sure the lodger boy doesn't mind giving up his room for me?

YVONNE: It was Lip's idea.

SYLVIA: Lip. – What an unusual name.

YVONNE: It's short for Phillip.

SYLVIA: That's my son-in-law's name. – I think I'll go and see them tomorrow. My family.

YVONNE: That'll be nice.

SYLVIA: Probably not.

YVONNE: How come?

SYLVIA: I've got a lot of stuff to make up for. And not very much time.

YVONNE: Time?

SYLVIA: The doctor, he says I've got dementia. My pal, Jean, she got it. Three weeks after she was diagnosed, she didn't know if it was Pancake Tuesday or Sheffield Wednesday.

YVONNE: Poor Jean.

SYLVIA: Six months later. Dead and buried. I just need to right some of the wrongs while I can still remember them.

YVONNE: Well, you're welcome to stay here for as long as you need to.

(YVONNE goes to leave.)

SYLVIA: My Yvonne, she was beautiful. Bright blue eyes. Spitting image of my father. – I never really was a good mother. The stuff I did. – The stuff I ignored. It's unforgivable. – My Yvonne, she looked so much like my father – I detested him. So, I never really made that connection with her. – That bond. She never really felt like my daughter. The apple of her father's eye though. She could do no wrong, and when he died, I couldn't even look at her. Everything she did, every move she made just reminded me of him. It was heart breaking. Then. – A few years later, I found a new man. It all happened so quickly and before I knew it Michael was living with us. Six months later, that's when he started. He would start coming to bed later and later. I heard him climb into my daughter's bed. – I knew what was happening, but I just rolled over in bed and forced myself to sleep. I don't know why. She just had those eyes. My father's eyes. He was evil, and I just wanted to punish him, so I punished her. – Punished her because of my dad and because my husband loved her more than he could've ever loved me. I really wasn't a good mother, you know. That's why I haven't seen her in so long. – That's why I told her I was living in Portugal. *(Pause.)* God, you don't know how long I've kept that to myself. It feels good to tell someone, you know.

YVONNE: What would you have done if they, your family just turned up to visit you?

SYLVIA: They wouldn't have. My son-in-law – he's a waster. Spends most of his time nursing a can of cheap lager or propping up a bar. They've not got two pennies to rub together. I never had to worry about them turning up on the doorstep. I've given Yvonne enough bad memories to last a lifetime, and most of them happened in her own home. She wasn't going to come looking for more. You know, I haven't seen my family in over eighteen years. I just knew that it was probably best for me to stay away. I've got a grandson, you know. Eighteen years old – I know I don't look old enough to have a grandson that age, but I do. – Never even met the poor boy.

YVONNE: The lad can't miss what he's never had. – I tell you what, why don't you get your head down for a few hours. I'm sure you've had a long day. And then, after you've had a nap, we can see about finding your family.

SYLVIA: That sounds good. I've missed them. Been a while. Maybe I should've told them I was coming. What do you think I should do?

YVONNE: I don't really know what to say to you. – Maybe this time it'll be different.

(SYLVIA *goes to her handbag.*)

SYLVIA: I'm sure I might have their phone number in here somewhere. *(She pulls out her diary and hands it to* YVONNE.*)* Here, it's a landline number though.

YVONNE: Let's see then.

SYLVIA: You're from around here. Do you recognise any of the numbers?

YVONNE: I don't. Sorry. I'm sure we'll be able to find your family soon. They must've lived around here for a while. I'm sure someone must know where they live.

SYLVIA: I hope so.

YVONNE: So do I.

(There is a change in SYLVIA.*)*

SYLVIA: Thank you for letting me stay, Yvonne. I know I haven't been the best mam. But you've been a good daughter today.

YVONNE: Just shout if you need anything. Good night, Mam.

SYLVIA: Can you do me a favour?

YVONNE: Of course.

SYLVIA: Get rid of this for me.

*(*SYLVIA *takes off her wedding ring and hands it to* YVONNE, *who doesn't take the ring.)*

YVONNE: We can talk about this in the morning.

SYLVIA: No, no. I know now, take it. Throw it. Pawn it. I don't care. I don't need anything from him, from Michael. –

Besides, it'll be your father waiting for me when I get to the Pearly Gates. Not him.

*(*YVONNE *takes the ring and goes to walk away.)*

YVONNE: I'm going to bed.

(There is another change in SYLVIA.*)*

SYLVIA: Good night. Do you think we could go and find Yvonne tomorrow? Her baby should be due any day.

(We switch focus back to the Kitchen. PHILLIP *and* RHONDA*'s whisky bottle is significantly emptier.)*

RHONDA: So, Phillip. Why have I never had a request from you?

PHILLIP: I'm a happily married man, Rhonda.

RHONDA: I meant from my catalogues.

PHILLIP: Has she put you up to this? If I've told her once, I've told her a hundred times. I am not going to let her stick a dildo up my arse, right! It's not my thing. I've heard the stories! I go down the Pub! We all know why Skinny Simon walks around the Pub with a limp on a Saturday. We all know that Pork Pie Pat is shoving all sorts up him.

RHONDA: Yvonne's asked you to stick a dildo up your arse?

PHILLIP: Yes! And I am telling you! It's not for me.

RHONDA: You need to be more open, Phillip. You can be sexually free!

PHILLIP: I am sexually comfortable, thank you very much!

(Blackout.)

Scene Nine
Tuesday. 10AM. The Kitchen.

*(*PHILLIP, SYLVIA, *and* YVONNE *are all sitting at the table eating breakfast.* LIP *enters.)*

YVONNE: Morning, son.

LIP: Morning.

*(*LIP *sits down.)*

YVONNE: Rhonda was around again this morning.

PHILLIP: I hope you didn't give her anything else.

YVONNE: Gary's doing another sponsored event.

LIP: What's he doing now?

YVONNE: God knows.

PHILLIP: Remember when he ran that fun run dressed as a bottle of Lucozade for all of the people in the county that were being verbally abused by their parrots?

*(*LIP *imitates a parrot physically and audibly.)*

LIP: Fat bastard. Specky prick.

PHILLIP: One year, I remember he ate nothing but dog food for a week.

LIP: That was just a protest because the Blockbusters down by the precinct weren't ordering Marmaduke on DVD.

YVONNE: He wanted to shave his head too. I can't remember what for. But Rhonda wouldn't let him because she didn't want to be married to a Phil Mitchell look-a-like.

PHILLIP: Ay, son! I saw you hurrying that tidy bit of skirt out the door this morning. – Nice work, son. Just like your old man.

SYLVIA: Phillip, do you have to be so vulgar around the breakfast table?

PHILLIP: Come on, Sylvia…

SYLVIA: I would prefer to wait until after I've eaten my grapefruit to hear your sexist remarks about that young girl, who might I add is probably half your age.

LIP: What even is a grapefruit? Where did you even get one from around here?

SYLVIA: Would you like to try a segment?

LIP: No, I'm alright, thanks.

YVONNE: So, that girl from this morning. Was that Rosie, then? The *famous* Rosie?

LIP: No, Mam. That was Anna.

SYLVIA: Lovely.

(YVONNE is clearly annoyed by the fact that LIP *has multiple sexual partners, but she tries to remain calm.)*

YVONNE: Toast? – Mother? Phil? Lip?

(YVONNE stands up.)

PHILLIP: You couldn't stick the kettle on as well could you, love? I'm gaspin'.

YVONNE: So, Anna, eh? Where did you meet this *lovely* Anna?

LIP: At Ben's house party.

PHILLIP: You know, two sugars…

YVONNE: Ben's house party was only last Friday – So, have you told Anna or Rosie about your grand plans to go off fighting for Queen and country in Afghanistan?

SYLVIA: Oh, the army? That is a fine career choice for a strapping, young lad like yourself.

YVONNE: Not now, Mother! *(Pause.)* So, have ya?

LIP: They both know that I'm not looking for anything long term.

SYLVIA: Now you're starting to sound like your old man, bar the accent.

YVONNE: I SAID NOT NOW!

LIP: I don't see what the big deal is.

YVONNE: I don't think that it's right. Does the other girl know that you've been sleeping with this Anna girl?

SYLVIA: Honey, I may be old, and my time may have passed. But, if the boy is telling us that he isn't looking for anything long term, then I'll bet my signed photo of Laurence Olivier that those two girls know nothing about each other.

YVONNE: Are you trying to put me in an early grave? Phillip, are you going to say something?

(PHILLIP *is sitting there with a massive smile plastered across his face.*)

PHILLIP: What do you want me to say? He's a teenager for crying out loud, of course he's going to be out there shagging everything that moves!

YVONNE: Oh my God! You're enjoying this aren't you? You're proud of him! You're proud of your son degrading women.

PHILLIP: You can pack it in with the whole 'holier than thou' routine, love. You weren't a virgin when you were his age.

LIP: These family gatherings are getting more and more uncomfortable for me.

PHILLIP: Ignore your Mam, Son.

SYLVIA: Right, Lip. My only grandchild…

(RHONDA *enters, hungover and wearing large sunglasses.*)

RHONDA: Morning everybody!

ALL: Morning!

RHONDA: You don't happen to have a spare drop of milk, do you? Gary's used the last of it. He's just had to nip down to the Mayor's Office to drop off some sponsor money. You know, from last night, he did the sponsored singathon to Songs of Praise for all the sex addicts in the local area. It went really well apparently!

SYLVIA: Oh, I love Songs of Praise.

YVONNE: Lovely – There's a carton in the fridge, just take it.

RHONDA: Oh, Yvonne. Are you sure?

YVONNE: Yes! There's two in there.

RHONDA: You are a lifesaver, Yvonne. I'll get you one back! See you later, Lip.

(RHONDA *hurries out.*)

PHILLIP: Of course she'll get us one back.

SYLVIA: As I was saying, Lip. My only grandchild! What do you want to do today? By the looks of it, I have a lot of birthdays and Christmases to make up for.

YVONNE: Mam, you don't have to do that.

SYLVIA: I want to spoil my Grandson…

YVONNE: Sorry, Mam. Lip's busy today. Rhonda asked if he would help fix her fence.

SYLVIA: Her who just came for the milk? The woman with all the dogs?

LIP: I'm alright. I'll pass.

YVONNE: She said she'd pay you thirty quid.

LIP: *(Very quickly.)* Sorry Grandma.

SYLVIA: Another day then!

YVONNE: Well, I thought that maybe you and I could spend some time together today, Mam?

SYLVIA: We could! We could go and buy some baby clothes, and I've been meaning to get my hair cut!

YVONNE: I'll cut it for you when we get back if you want.

SYLVIA: I would love for you to cut my hair.

YVONNE: Right, well let's get to the shops and I'll do it later.

PHILLIP: What about me?

YVONNE: I'm sure the bar in The Fox and Hounds needs propping up.

PHILLIP: A very apt suggestion, Yvonne.

YVONNE: Lip, you better get ready. I told Rhonda that you would be over for eleven.

LIP: Right.

PHILLIP: Are sure you don't want me to come on your shopping trip?

YVONNE: Phillip…

(YVONNE *is interrupted by* SYLVIA.)

SYLVIA: Here, take this. (SYLVIA *hands* PHILLIP *a ten-pound note.*) Make yourself scarce.

PHILLIP: Thanks, Sylvia. But this will only just pay off my tick bill.

YVONNE: PHILLIP!

PHILLIP: Right! I'm going!

YVONNE: You too, Lip. Go and get dressed. I'll clean this up. Mother, you can go through and watch the television if you want.

SYLVIA: No, no. I'll help you.

(Blackout.)

Scene Ten
Tuesday. 3PM. The Kitchen.

(YVONNE is sitting at the kitchen table, crying. There is a utility bill sitting on the table in front of her. SYLVIA enters carrying bags of shopping.)

SYLVIA: What's the matter, love?

YVONNE: Nothing. I'm just being silly.

SYLVIA: Come on, you can tell me. Nobody sits at the table crying over nothing.

(SYLVIA sits down.)

YVONNE: I think Phillip's having an affair.

SYLVIA: Well, have you caught him with another woman?

YVONNE: No.

SYLVIA: Well then, what makes you think he's having an affair?

YVONNE: Last night, Phillip told me that he's been going down the Pub every night, but I went down the pub today because they have those scampi flavoured crisps that I've been craving. And I've been quite friendly with Cilla, one of the barmaids in the past.

(SYLVIA interrupts YVONNE.)

SYLVIA: And what's she got to do with any of this? Is she the tart he's having it off with?

YVONNE: No! I was down the pub and we were having a laugh and a bit of chat and I said to her, "I hope my Phillip was behaving in here." – And then she said, "he hasn't been in here since Saturday night." That were three nights ago!

SYLVIA: So, what? We can rule out last night, because he was here. Just because he's not telling you where he's going, that doesn't mean he's having an affair.

YVONNE: Then, the landline bill came through this morning, and I was looking through the call logs. There's this one number that keeps popping up all over the history. See! The one ending in nine-oh-nine!

SYLVIA: A phone number could be anyone! Ring the number, see who answers the phone!

YVONNE: I can't do that! What if Phillip's with them now. I haven't seen him all day.

SYLVIA: Give me the number.

(SYLVIA *pulls her mobile out and dials the number from the piece of paper.*)

YVONNE: Don't, Mother!

SYLVIA: Sssh!

(SYLVIA puts the phone on speakerphone, and it rings until it goes to voicemail. NICKY's voicemail plays as a sound effect.)

NICKY'S VOICEMAIL: *"Hello, hello! You've reached Nicky! Unfortunately, Nicky can't reach you right now, not to worry though; the throws of our modern society means I won't be away from my phone for much longer! Leave me a message and I'll try and get back, right as soon as I can!"*

YVONNE: It's a woman!

SYLVIA: Yes, I heard.

YVONNE: Hang up, don't leave a message.

(The end of NICKY's voicemail plays, ending with a beep, and SYLVIA lifts the phone to her mouth.)

SYLVIA: Listen here, bitch! I'm going to find you!

(YVONNE tries to disguise her voice with a really bad Scottish accent.)

YVONNE: HANG UP!

SYLVIA: What's the matter with your voice?

(YVONNE keeps using a fake voice.)

YVONNE: HANG UP!

(SYLVIA does so.)

SYLVIA: Do you want a glass of water?

*(*YVONNE's *voice goes back to normal.)*

YVONNE: No, I'm fine.

SYLVIA: What was that voice?

YVONNE: Didn't want her to recognise me!

(SYLVIA laughs. Her tone changes almost straight away though.)

SYLVIA: Well, Yvonne, love. I don't really know what to say to you. But whoever this Nicky woman is, I don't really fancy your chances, darling.

YVONNE: So, you think it too? You think he's having an affair?

SYLVIA: I think so, love.

YVONNE: What am I going to do, Mam? I've got a baby on the way! I've got a baby on the way and my husband's going to leave me for some tart called Nicky! And then, my other baby thinks it's a good idea to go running off to the army, and what about if he dies?

(A pause.)

SYLVIA: Hang on a minute! Have you washed Phillip's jeans? The ones he was wearing yesterday.

YVONNE: No. They're still in the basket.

SYLVIA: Go and get them.

YVONNE: What have Phil's dirty jeans got to do with anything?

SYLVIA: The man isn't all there! I've always said that he was a few cigarettes short of a packet!

YVONNE: You're making no sense. *(YVONNE pulls the jeans out of the washing basket.)* Here.

(SYLVIA empties the pockets of the jeans.)

SYLVIA: Lighter, empty fag packet, betting slip.

(YVONNE picks up the betting slip.)

YVONNE: This betting slip isn't from the shop in the Precinct. Phillip usually goes to the Bookies in the Precinct. This is for the one down by the Community Centre. The one down by that brand-new block of flats!

SYLVIA: Come on then!

YVONNE: What?

SYLVIA: Let's go down there.

YVONNE: Loads of students have just moved into that block of flats! Did she, on the voicemail, did she sound like a student?

SYLVIA: Get your boxing gloves out, Lady!

*(*SYLVIA *exits.)*

YVONNE: Mam, you can't be serious!

SYLVIA: *(Off-stage.)* Come on.

YVONNE: But…

SYLVIA: *(Off-stage.)* Hurry up, Yvonne.

YVONNE: Oh, alright. I'll need to write a note for Lip.

*(*YVONNE *writes on a post-it note* and *exits, with her handbag. Blackout.)*

Scene Eleven

Tuesday. 3.30PM. The Community Centre.

(The stage curtains are closed. YVONNE and SYLVIA enter. There are two signs pinned to the stage curtains. One reads: 'Anger Management', and the other says, 'Life Modelling'.)

YVONNE: *(Off-stage.)* Mam, this is useless.

(SYLVIA enters.)

SYLVIA: Come on, Yvonne. That man in the bookies said he saw Phillip come in here half an hour ago. – He's got to be in one of these rooms.

(SYLVIA pokes her head through the stage curtains, below the Anger Management sign. She doesn't notice the sign.)

YVONNE: You can't just go peeping into rooms.

(SYLVIA still has her head inside the curtains.)

SYLVIA: Phillip? – No, Yvonne. He's not in here. Just a bunch of lunatics punching pillows in here.

OFF-STAGE SHOUTING: PISS OFF, SHORT ARSE!

(YVONNE pulls SYLVIA away from the curtain and points to the sign above her.)

YVONNE: Mother! That is the anger management class!

SYLVIA: Oh well, onto the next one.

YVONNE: No, Mam! That's a life drawing class!

SYLVIA: A what?

(SYLVIA pokes her head in.)

YVONNE: Someone's going to be naked in there! You can't just go barging in.

SYLVIA: Well, well, well. – Yvonne, you won't believe this.

YVONNE: What?

SYLVIA: It's Phillip. And he's naked.

YVONNE: Oh my god! OH MY GOD!

SYLVIA: Here, have a peek.

YVONNE: No, I can't. I don't want to see it. Oh my god I knew it.

SYLVIA: Well surely, you've seen it before and if I'm being honest darling – not bad.

YVONNE: Mam! Oh my god I knew it. Didn't I bloody say? And in the Community Centre of all places. *(YVONNE paces up and down in front the curtain.)* That dirty bastard. Why has he felt the need to do this, I'm very good to him at home if you know what I mean. Jesus, it's because I'm pregnant, isn't it? No one is attracted to a pregnant lump. Well, he should've thought of that –

SYLVIA: Yvonne love, it's not what you think. Here, have a look.

(YVONNE stops pacing and stares at the curtain. She sighs and takes a look through the curtain.)

YVONNE: OH MY GOD, PHILLIP!

(YVONNE bursts through the curtain and the stage curtains are opened fully for the audience to see. PHILLIP is standing completely naked surrounded by artists, all standing behind an easel. There is a bowl of grapes covering his penis. Everyone in the circle stops and turns to look at YVONNE and SYLVIA who have now burst through the curtain.)

PHILLIP: Oh god. Yvonne, love.

YVONNE: Phillip?

PHILLIP: I can explain.

SYLVIA: Probably a good idea.

PHILLIP: Alright Sylvia?

(There is a long pause. PHILLIP and YVONNE stare at each other in disbelief, no one speaks. Eventually NICKY steps out from behind her easel and smiles broadly.)

NICKY: Yvonne, how lovely to have you here during our class.

YVONNE: Class?

NICKY: Live art. Isn't your husband's body just marvellous. He has kindly agreed to be our muse. Please feel free to walk around and observe our student's work. I think you will be pleasantly surprised with the results.

*(*YVONNE *stays still for a moment and then slowly begins to walk around the circle, stopping to glance at the different canvases.* PHILLIP *is noticeably uncomfortable and stays frozen in the centre of the circle.* SYLVIA *also walks around, viewing the art.)*

NICKY: You will notice that no two canvases are the same. Everyone here has drawn inspiration from your husband in a different way, choosing a different focus and letting the art tell the rest of the story. Isn't it marvellous?

YVONNE: Yes – marvellous.

SYLVIA*: (Stopping at one of the canvases.)* Peachy.

YVONNE: So, all of this is just art. Nothing else?

NICKY: Well, there's no such thing as just art – *(*YVONNE *shoots* NICKY *an icy look.)* But yes. Just art in here. A safe space for my students to let creativity flow and for your husband to appreciate himself in a new light.

PHILLIP: Come on, love. I've done a good thing here.

YVONNE: I'm glad you're not having an affair.

PHILLIP: What? Of course, I'm not. You thought I was shagging someone else?

NICKY: Okay class! I think that's enough for today. Thank you for all of your hard work, we have some fantastic pieces of art emerging. And let's give a huge thank you to Phillip for agreeing to be the epicentre of our creative journey here today. Round of applause people!

(The room erupts into applause. PHILLIP gives an awkward bow.)

NICKY: Alright people! Let's get cleaned off and let our muse gather himself. It was lovely to officially meet you and congratulations to you both for the scrumptious bundle of joy that is about to enter your lives.

(NICKY shakes hands with YVONNE and SYLVIA and then exits. The rest of the class follow her lead. PHILLIP remains standing behind the bowl of grapes.)

PHILLIP: I'm sorry, I should have told you.

YVONNE: Yes, you should have. I was going crazy thinking you had another woman.

SYLVIA: I'm just going to wait outside.

(SYLVIA exits. But, she accidentally enters the Anger Management class again.)

OFF-STAGE SHOUTING: WHAT DID I TELL YOU? PISS OFF!

(SYLVIA *crosses the stage.*)

SYLVIA: Wrong way.

(SYLVIA *exits.*)

PHILLIP: Honestly, do you think I have the mental capacity to deal with two women? Yvonne, all that arty talk, it's a lot of shite. I get sixty quid a session. I was trying to get some extra cash together and I was going to surprise you with a cot for the baby.

YVONNE: How many sessions have you done?

PHILLIP: Four. Got a good bit put away now. Of course, I had to take my cut for a few beers.

YVONNE: Phil. This is one of the nicest things you've ever done. I love you.

PHILLIP: Pass me the husband of the year award…

YVONNE: Don't push it. I thought you were off shagging that arty-farty woman.

PHILLIP: God no.

YVONNE: What am I gonna do with you? *(She eats one of the grapes from the bowl.)* Come on, let's go home. I've got my own picture I'd like to paint.

PHILLIP: Anything for you.

YVONNE: Make sure you bring those grapes. – *(To herself.)* And I need to apologise to Lip and you need to clean the bath out.

PHILLIP: Why?

(PHILLIP lifts the bowl of grapes and exits through the curtain, covering himself with a towel. Blackout.)

Scene Twelve
Wednesday. 10AM. The Kitchen

(YVONNE and SYLVIA are folding washing. RHONDA enters.)

RHONDA: Morning, only me.

YVONNE: Morning, love. Everything okay?

RHONDA: Everything's fine. I was just popping…

(SYLVIA holds out a pair of knickers. They're huge, much too large for anyone to fit into them.)

SYLVIA: Fuck me. – Who's are these?

YVONNE: They are my maternity knickers, Mother!

(YVONNE grabs the knickers and puts them back in the washing basket.)

RHONDA: I was just popping over to see if Lip wanted to help Gary fix the fence again? Gary wanted to ask Lip before paying someone else to do it.

SYLVIA: Our Lip just fixed your fence yesterday! Surely if it's already broken – he must've done a shite job. So why have him fix it again?

RHONDA: Someone broke in again. Trying to get at the dogs.

YVONNE: Jesus! – Do you want a cup of tea?

RHONDA: Sounds good.

SYLVIA: You wouldn't have this problem if you bred German Shepherds. They'd rip them limb from limb.

(YVONNE *interrupts her.*)

YVONNE: Mother, don't you have something you could be doing right now?

SYLVIA: Actually, I was thinking of writing to my sister.

YVONNE: You should. I think Aunty June would appreciate a letter.

SYLVIA: I think I will. – See you later, Rhonda.

RHONDA: See you later.

(SYLVIA *exits.*)

YVONNE: Are you not getting worried? That's the third time in two weeks.

RHONDA: Nah, I'm not worried. Gary's bought a baseball bat. – How's your mam? She alright?

YVONNE: She's never been alright – I've no real clue what's going on. I don't really think she knows either, she keeps dipping in and out. Doesn't know who I am, or where she is, or what year it is. Then, the next minute she knows everything.

RHONDA: Christ. And what about you, how are you handling everything?

YVONNE: I'm alright. I've spoken to her a couple of times when she's been aware. I think we're finally sorting through some of our issues.

RHONDA: That's good to hear!

YVONNE: And Phillip has been helping out more. Finally got the kick up the arse he needed. Things are looking up other than the fact I'm a fat cow and I can't tie my own shoelaces.

RHONDA: Don't be silly love, you look –

YVONNE: Don't you fucking dare.

RHONDA: Sorry you're right. You're a fucking whale. Actually. I meant to ask you. Do you fancy sponsoring Gary?

YVONNE: What's he doing now? He bloody loves these sponsors.

RHONDA: Him and the other lads down at the Working Men's Club, you know the one on Bricklethwaite Road – Well, they are doing a sponsored sing-along of the High School Musical soundtrack for thirty-two hours for all the little chaps in the area with OCD.

YVONNE: Right.

RHONDA: Poor bastards, Yvonne – I tell ya. Can't go out of the house without turning the lights on and off fourteen times.

YVONNE: Right. – Put us down for twenty pence an hour.

RHONDA: Brilliant! Thanks Yvonne.

YVONNE: Has he got many sponsors?

RHONDA: Yeah, him and the lads are doing all right. They were doing the rounds last night, asking at all the shops at the precinct.

YVONNE: That's good then, tell him I said good luck.

RHONDA: Will do. – Right, I better be off. Get round and check on him. When I left, he was doing some sort of voice warm up. Driving the dogs fucking mental. See you later.

(RHONDA exits. YVONNE moves off stage and comes back immediately with a large picture frame shaped package wrapped in brown paper and leans it against the table. She sits at the kitchen table.)

YVONNE: PHILLIP, COME HERE A MINUTE.

(PHILLIP enters.)

PHILLIP: What is it?

YVONNE: Here, I bought you a present.

PHILLIP: What? You shouldn't have.

YVONNE: Honestly, you've been surprisingly helpful while I've been pregnant. So, I thought I would get you a little something to remind you what a good husband you can be when you want to be.

PHILLIP: You really didn't have to.

YVONNE: I know, I wanted to. I thought we could put it up in the Living Room, above the telly.

PHILLIP: I'm so lucky to have you.

YVONNE: Go on then, open it.

(As PHILLIP *rips off the brown paper* LIP *enters.)*

LIP: Alright?

*(*PHILLIP *finishes ripping off the brown paper, to reveal one of the paintings from* NICKY's *class. In the painting,* PHILLIP *is naked with the grapes covering his penis.)*

YVONNE: Well. What do you think?

LIP: Are you mental?

PHILLIP: Yvonne, love…

YVONNE: This was the best one. She gave it to me dead cheap; I really think that it would look good above the telly.

LIP: You're having a laugh!

YVONNE: We haven't got any art in the house. I thought I'd try to make the place a bit more civilised.

PHILLIP: This isn't the type of thing that I want everyone to see.

YVONNE: Do you not like it?

PHILLIP: I like it. As something for just the two of us. Not as a statement piece for the house.

YVONNE: Well now I feel silly.

PHILLIP: Maybe we could put it above the bed?

YVONNE: Really?

PHILLIP: Of course!

LIP: What are you playing at? Posing with your dick out.

PHILLIP: Like your mother said, it's art. Something civilised. Not that you would know anything about that sort of thing.

YVONNE: It's perfectly natural, when you're in a loving relationship. To explore other things. Sexually.

LIP: The pair of you are messed up in the head.

PHILLIP: Speaking of love lives, how are the two birds you're shagging?

(LIP *doesn't answer.*)

YVONNE: Has something happened?

PHILLIP: By the looks of it, his threesome's turned into a wank.

LIP: What is wrong with you?

PHILLIP: Not such a cocky, little twat anymore.

YVONNE: That's enough Phillip.

PHILLIP: Look son, it was bound to come crashing down at one point! Just be thankful that you got your end away for as long as you did! Let's be honest, you're not that much of a looker anyway, so be extra grateful it lasted as long as it did!

YVONNE: PHILLIP! ENOUGH!

LIP: Fuck the both of you!

*(*LIP *exits.)*

YVONNE: Well, you handled that marvellously.

PHILLIP: Yvonne.

YVONNE: Not now.

*(*YVONNE *chases after* LIP. *Blackout.)*

Scene Thirteen
Wednesday. 1PM. The Kitchen.

*(*SYLVIA *is sitting at the table.* YVONNE *enters. She looks smarter than usual; she's wearing a shirt and smart trousers.)*

SYLVIA: You're looking smart.

YVONNE: Thanks.

SYLVIA: Who's funeral?

YVONNE: What?

SYLVIA: Nothing.

YVONNE: Listen, can you stay in the house for a couple of hours? Lip's away playing football and he's left his keys, wallet and his inhaler. I would stay myself, but I've got a job interview down at the Post Office at two and then I've got an appointment with my doctor right after that.

SYLVIA: It's not like I'm going anywhere.

YVONNE: Great.

SYLVIA: Do you think it's wise? For you to be going to a job interview. – When, you know – you're about to have a baby.

YVONNE: We need the money. More mouths to feed.

SYLVIA: I don't think you should be working in your condition.

YVONNE: I'm pregnant, Mother! I'm not dying.

SYLVIA: Well, make sure that the Post Office know that you're pregnant! You can't be doing any heavy lifting.

*(*YVONNE *points to her baby bump.)*

YVONNE: I think it's pretty obvious!

SYLVIA: Well, people don't like to assume. Do they? They might just think you're a fat bastard…' Just make sure, if you get the job. – Just make sure they know – I mean, love. You're no spring chicken. People won't assume that a woman your age is pregnant, will they?

YVONNE: I'm not quite over the hill yet.

SYLVIA: You're reaching the top of it though.

YVONNE: It's a bit too late in life for you to start playing the role of the concerned parent!

SYLVIA: I thought that we put all of that business behind us?

YVONNE: That doesn't automatically allow you to start being overprotective. I'm old enough to know how to take care of myself!

SYLVIA: I know – I'm just. –

YVONNE: Just don't!

SYLVIA: Yvonne. –

YVONNE: Don't! I'm nervous enough.

(YVONNE exits and enters again with her jacket; she's coming for her bag that's on the table.)

SYLVIA: Good luck.

(LIP enters.)

LIP: Mam.

YVONNE: Hello, son!

LIP: Mam. Brian offered me a job. – Coaching football!

YVONNE: That's good.

LIP: I've got to sign up for the training course though. But they do that at the College in Town, so that's no bother.

YVONNE: Honestly son, I'm dead chuffed for you, I am. But I really don't think now's the right time. With this little one on the way, we really can't afford for you to stop working at the shop. I'm sorry son, it just can't happen right now.

LIP: No, Mam. It's an apprenticeship. I'll get paid while I do it. It only pays a tenner less than the shop, but I'll still pay you the same.

YVONNE: Well, I suppose we could do that then. You'll have to tell Katrina though. And work your notice.

LIP: Fine.

YVONNE: Come here. *(*YVONNE *pulls* LIP *into a hug.)* I'm so proud of you son. Now you can leave all of that army stuff behind you and focus on this.

SYLVIA: Well done, son.

LIP: Thanks.

YVONNE: Well, this is a cause for a bit of a celebration, don't you think?

LIP: No. No more parties with condom balloons.

YVONNE: No, none of those. I was thinking tea down the pub tonight?

LIP: Sounds good.

YVONNE: Mam?

SYLVIA: No, no my love. I'm not feeling up to it. I'm due an early night tonight anyway. You go though, have a family night.

LIP: You are family.

SYLVIA: No, you don't want me spoiling it. Go off. Have some fun. Don't worry about me.

YVONNE: Only if you're sure?

SYLVIA: I'll be fine.

YVONNE: Right, Lip. I'm off. I'll be back around five, and then we'll go down the Pub.

(YVONNE and LIP exit. The stage fades to blackout. As the lights come back up, it's night-time. SYLVIA is the only one awake in the house. SYLVIA pulls an old, clunky video camera from one of her bags. She sets it up so that it is recording her face. She speaks directly into the camera.)

SYLVIA: Hello Yvonne, love. It's me; Sylvia, your mother. If you've been paying any attention to me, you'll know that I've not been right. My old noggin ain't what it used to be. And I want to end my time with you as me, and not as some silly, old bird drivelling nonsense. So, I want to start by saying I'm sorry. I'm sorry, Yvonne. I was a terrible mother. I never had the chance to tell you how sorry I was. You were just a little girl and I stood by and watched everything, because I wanted to punish you for something that you had nothing to do with. I said some pretty despicable things to you. When you told me, what Michael did to you, and I told you. – I told you that you were a liar and that I wished I never had you. I'm not going to lie to you, Yvonne. I'm ashamed of myself. I was wrong, Yvonne. I'm sorry. I stayed away for so long because I knew you were being looked after. I knew Phillip was taking care of you. – Phillip, you're a good man, regardless of how many times I've called you a waster. You have looked after my daughter more than I ever have. Thank you. Lip, you're a good boy, I really wish I hadn't waited eighteen years to be a grandma. Take care. Tell the new baby that I am sorry that they never got to meet their grandmother. But that was probably for the best. *(A pause.)* Well, t'ra then, I love you all.

*(*SYLVIA *turns the camera off and leaves with her suitcases. She leaves her jacket hanging on the back of the chair. Before she exits, she looks back for a final time, taking everything in. She exits. Blackout.)*

Epilogue

Wednesday. 11.45PM. Phillip and Yvonne's Bedroom.

(PHILLIP is sitting on the edge of the stage, as if he's leaning against the back door of the house. It's evident that he's drunk. He's clutching a can of lager.)

PHILLIP: *(To the audience.)* Who the fuck are you lot? Can't you see the sign outside? Grandma and Grandad are dead, so no telly – so we haven't got a fucking licence for one, alright? Now, piss off! *(Pause)* Not here about the telly licence? Get a fucking job then! Bunch of fucking layabouts. Alright – anyway. Moving on.

(There is a pause. He walks to the front of the stage.)

This is where we get off.

END OF PLAY

Printed in Great Britain
by Amazon

11273335R00078